The Dead Aviatrix

Spineless Wonders
PO Box 220
STRAWBERRY HILLS
New South Wales, Australia, 2012
shortaustralianstories.com.au

Text copyright © Carmel Bird 2017
Cover design by Bettina Kaiser
Typesetting by Heike Krieger | BKA+D
Published by Bronwyn Mehan. Assistant editors,
Jordan Meek and Siobhan Doig.

Typeset in Adobe Garamond Pro
Printed and bound by Ingram Spark
The Dead Aviatrix /Carmel Bird
ISBN 978-1-925052-76-3

Distribution in Australia and New Zealand by New South

A catalogue record for this book is available from the National Library of Australia

THE DEAD AVIATRIX

Eight Short Stories

CARMEL BIRD

Contents

The Dead Aviatrix and the Stratemyer Syndicate

The aviatrix sat looking on through all this tumult with a happy smile.

Now once upon a time – to tell the truth it was 1922 – there was a survey conducted in America. Yes, they checked out, I believe, the reading habits of 36,000 children and discovered that most of the books children were reading were produced by the Stratemeyer Syndicate. But the nature, and even the existence of the Syndicate didn't really become public until the late 1970s when the Syndicate was involved in a court case over copyright. The intelligent Edward Stratemeyer had realized that children were less interested in reading for moral instruction than in reading for thrills and pleasure. So he turned this realisation into a fortune based on an assembly line of millions of exciting stories, beginning in 1899 with *The Rover Boys*. And maybe you remember the Bobbsey Twins – they were Stratemeyer inventions. And Nancy Drew of course. Edward wrote under many pseudonyms, and he also had ghost writers who were sworn to secrecy.

Now one of the series, written under the name of Margaret Penrose, was *The Motor Girls*. Intrepid girls with cars. I am interested here in a title *The Gipsy Girl's Secret*. Here is the synopsis, short version:

'On a camping trip to the Adirondacks, the Motor Girls become involved in a mystery involving a Gypsy girl and a stolen purse.'

Quite a lot of involving there.

I set out to tell you the tale of the Dead Aviatrix, and in the process I discovered a quotation from The Gipsy Girl's Secret, and then I uncovered the fascinating history of the Stratemeyer Syndicate and became productively side-tracked. Anyhow, this was the quote:

'The aviatrix sat looking on through all this tumult with a happy smile.' I liked it – see above.

You don't often come across the word *aviatrix* you see. I have had half the title of this story you are reading for some years now, have had the story ready to tell, but it wasn't until I got onto Edward and his Syndicate that I discovered how to go about it. So that was a bit of a preamble. Here is the story. It's a publishing story.

Characters: Finch One (Aviatrix), Finch Two, Publishing Person, Airhead Intern, Ron.

I do apologise for the term *airhead*, but I don't know of an alternative that fits the case – well in fact I do know some, but airhead is the nicest.

Finch One, you will be happy to learn, was a famous Australian aviatrix. At last, the Aviatrix. Like the Motor Girls before her, she was intrepid, a flying pioneer. She was born five years after the Motor Girls made their appearance in *A Mystery of the Road*. And unlike the great and mysterious Amelia she did not disappear in the skies, but died in the fullness of time in 2009. Needless to say she produced an autobiography *The Flying Girl* which, while it did not attract those 36,000 American children, was a very pleasing account of a vital chapter in Australian history, and had a nice little echo of *The Flying Nun*. In her final years Finch One lived in a charming and romantic house that nestled in the trees at the top of a cliff looking down on the waters of Sydney Harbour. The only access to the house was by water, and by a long, steep unforgiving stone staircase. Finch One was ever agile, but you will probably have realized that.

Now while Finch One was happily fading away at the top of her pretty cliff, Finch Two was herself quite busy in her bushland retreat writing a book. Let's call this one *The Novel*. Matters were quite advanced, and Finch Two was waiting for the parcel in the mail that would be the final proofs for her attention. And they didn't come and they didn't come. Ron the postman would knock on the window of Finch Two's study, would hand in parcels of all kinds, and Finch Two would say to him – oh, nothing yet from the Publisher Person, is there, Ron? And Ron would open his eyes wide and say – No, Finch, nothing from there. And Finch Two would give him a chocolate anyway. So time went by and time went by, and one day, the PP took to the telephone and spoke sharply to Finch Two saying – So where are the proofs. We need to go to print tomorrow. We sent them three weeks ago.

NB: Finch One has died by this time.

And we are now involved in a bit of a mystery about the proofs.

So it is the time for a flashback. Remember that Intern? Airhead Intern? Yes, well there she was with a pile of parcels to take to the mail room. So much to think of, so much to do, tattoos to consider, a new bikini, an appointment with the footbinder etc etc. She quickly flew through the addresses on the database, attaching sticky labels to parcels, zip zip slip slop slap then off to the mailroom and out into the sunshine grab a coffee get the nails done sniff a little coke. Rave.

The manuscript of *The Novel* was, as you will have realized, addressed to Finch One, author of *The Flying Girl*, at the top of the winding stone stairs in the trees, on the cliff, looking over the sparkling waters of the celebrated Harbour. If Ron had been leaping up those stairs, he would have knocked on the window in vain. Alas, the parcel was, strangely, not returned to sender. Could it be that Airhead had not registered a return address? This is possible. Probable. There is, at the end of the rainbow, a place called the Dead Letter Office. And there the proofs of *The Novel* reside to this day.

PP got cracking, and new proofs were sent to Finch Two under the personal supervision of PP to the trusty hands of Ron who duly delivered them to the window of the studio, and in due course *The Novel* was published as if by magic. Airhead was awarded a PhD in Writing and Editing, and went on to become an important person in the mysterious world of publishing. The Aviatrix sat looking down on all this tumult, from her gallant machine in the sky, with a happy smile.

The Whirligigge of Time Brings In His Revenges

It was in the nineties that Frankie left Australia and went to Paris to study. She worked as an au pair, studied at the Sorbonne. Her special interests were the novels of Albert Camus and the works of Paul Claudel. She was born on the day (February 23, 1975) that Claudel died, although twenty years later. She was the kind of person who can see significance in such small coincidences, and she wrote a magnificent doctoral thesis taking in the work of both writers – no mean feat. Talk about analysis – this girl was, for a time, where critical analysis was *at*. (Dr Frances Mary Gellibrand, descendant of the first Attorney-General of Van Diemen's Land – it rhymes. He was the one who went exploring on the great big mainland of Australia and became lost and was never heard of again.) Frankie married her professor (Jean-Luc) had two children (Coco and Gigi), lived in a rather glamorous apartment in the sixteenth (close to the Parc Monceau where there was for a time a pretty carousel), and became a successful advertising copywriter. This is all sounding good. Lived happily ever after, as it happened. But there must be more to it than this. Fear not.

OK, so advertising was her profession, but she also wrote a couple of novels. There you have it. Like her ancestor who dissolved in the wilds of Victoria, the first novel was published but then disappeared without trace. Oh, and she wrote a play and quite a few poems, but the focus here is actually going to be on the second novel. It was the novel that, in 2017, won first prize in one of the hundreds of important (they call them *prestigious*) literary awards in her country of birth. It was what is called a 'manuscript award'. Instead of entering a book for a prize, you enter the manuscript of an unpublished book. Then the winning book gets published and the winning author probably gets some prize money as well. (Frankie did, and she bought some fabulous new curtains for the dining room as well as a family holiday in Provence.)

The history of this novel (*The Heat of Summer*) is the real subject of my tale. That, and the wheel of fortune and the quirks of fate. The book takes its first inspiration from Camus' famous *L'Etranger*, and its content is drawn from the aforementioned history of Joseph Tice Gellibrand, the disappearing Attorney-General of Van Diemen's Land. Well, you can see that what Frankie was doing here was risky. It was what is often described as *literary fiction.*

Unwisely perhaps, Frankie did not use an agent, but submitted her book to publishers herself. The manuscript was ignored by three publishers who did not respond in any way to Frankie's emailed submission. It was rejected by three more, for, as they all explained, they could not find a place for it in their list. All this is perfectly normal and understandable, for publishers seldom have time to read more than the synopsis, if that, of an *unsolicited manuscript* found in what they ominously term the *slush pile.* And Frankie's brief synopsis, as you can imagine, was unusual and a bit alarming – something along the lines of:

'In the heat of summer, 21 February 1837, two real life explorers, George Hesse and Joseph Gellibrand set off on horseback to travel through the forest from Geelong to Melbourne, and they disappeared forever leaving no trace. These men are the inspiration for the protagonists. The novel references the work of Albert Camus, in particular *L'Etranger* in which the intense heat and light of the sun dominate the consciousness and reason of the protagonist. Chapters alternate between Algerian scenes of violence, and episodes of gothic violence in the Victorian bushland where the two men encounter not only hostile native groups, but also two cannibal felons who have inhabited the region for several years.' You know the sort of thing. But for some reason, the judges of the manuscript prize fixed upon *The Heat of Summer* as THEIR WINNER. I believe it was well written, if that is a criterion. (Perhaps the other entries were even stranger. Less literary, more literary? Who knows?) Anyhow, failing to make any headway with the publishers, Frankie entered it for the manuscript prize, and you know the rest – the curtains, the holiday, the publication.

However as it happens there is more. Back when the manuscript was hanging about in slush piles, it caught the eye of at least one publisher (she, Lydia O'Hara, was at Chekhov and Chekhov) who, tired and frazzled and in need of a drink and a joke late one Friday afternoon, idly posted a note about this novel on social media. This was a kind of odd thing to do really. Whatever happened to empathy and privacy and decency, you might wonder. Publishers may certainly mock the slush pile among themselves, for heaven knows they have a lot to put up with. But mocking the specifics of your slush on social media seems to me (naïve!) to be taking nastiness a bit too far.

'Today's slush pile reveals this jewel – a novel that references the work of Camus while dealing with native groups and cannibal felons in the Victorian bush. French absurd meets Australian gothic!' And the other publishers joined in with glee, further mocking the hapless novel from the murky slush pile with their comments, and ticking the handy little like button to show solidarity with the poor tired publisher at Chekhov and Chekhov in need of a nice stiff drink. (I don't need to tell you that the company was laughingly known in the industry as Fuckoff and Fuckoff.)

As far as I know Frankie never saw all this, for social media melts away in one direction, even though it also lurks around forever in another. That's not the issue here. But what is of interest is that fact that the designated publisher of the prizewinning manuscript was, yes, Chekhov and Chekhov. That's irony for you, isn't it.

So there's Lydia O'Hara in her office one hot Friday afternoon in February, receiving the interesting news that she's going to publish the winning manuscript which is called *The Heat of Summer*. It's a good two years since the little social media glitch, and in fact, Lydia has no recollection of it at all. The media hype for *The Heat of Summer* is huge, what with the glamour of Frankie's Paris life, and the deep fascination with gothic Australian bush stuff and so forth. *Based around the tragic life of her ancestor.* Smash hit. Frankie turned out to be a publicist's dream, having, as well as the attributes I have alluded to, long legs, a face that could sell cosmetics and airline tickets, and an engaging lisp. A picture of her with Jean-Luc and the children at the carousel in the Parc Monceau practically went viral. Her older novel that disappeared so long ago is due to be revised and resurrected, with a generous Introduction by a very well known Parisian novelist. Frankie is, as they say, *working on a new manuscript,* a book of essays, ranging in subject matter from pre-historic Antarctica to space travel, to the changing climate of the Earth, to the poetry of Paul Claudel. What's more she has become even more successful in her work as a copywriter. Win, win.

Yes, *The Heat of Summer* is going to be a movie.

The whirligigge of time[1] has done its work, the wheel of fortune has turned, and all's well that ends well, provided that it ends. 'And Time will pardon Paul Claudel, Pardons him for writing well[2].'

---

1   *Twelfth Night*
2   W.H.Auden, *In Memory of W.B. Yeats*

Cold Case

When I was a child I used to pick flowers from the edges of gardens and take them home and treasure them. It was harmless enough. Once I went stealing apples with a boy, and a man chased us off with a gun.

In Australian country towns in the nineteen fifties you didn't get many murders, and those you did get were generally solved quickly and easily. In my town, eight-year-old Daphne Harrower was found strangled in the golden gorse at the top of the quarry, her mouth stuffed with the pale green blossoms of the snowball bush. They never found the killer. She had not been sexually molested. It's one of those cold cases that are sometimes featured on television, families never giving up hope, sad black and white photographs hovering for a moment on the screen, then fading again from memory, sliding back into the swamp of history.

I remember the shock and the hushed tones. The creepy satisfaction in the assurance that she had not been *interfered with*. Even at the time this euphemism struck me as strange. Strangling her and stuffing her mouth with green flowers seemed to be a pretty serious interference. The smudged photographs on the front of the newspaper – a sinister picture of the quarry, a picture of Daphne smiling, standing by the curly iron gate in front of her house, wearing a floral dress and white socks and lace-up shoes, probably brown. She had a big ribbon bow on one side of her head. Her hair was curled, the newspaper said that it was ginger. The picture had been taken the day before she was killed. You can see the house behind her is one of those Spanish style ones that were popular in Australia in the thirties, a kind of Californian influence. A crazy pavement winds back from the gate to the house where Daphne has had, the paper says, Kellogg's Corn Flakes, a glass of milk and a piece of toast and Vegemite.

I never knew Daphne, she lived on the other side of the town, but she became part of the fabric of everybody's life, part of the legend of the town, the dead girl in the gorse bushes up on the quarry, the girl with the snowball flowers in her mouth. I could have been that girl.

Like every other child in the town I identified with Daphne. I imagined my own photograph at our gate in front of our house, smiling for the last time because I was about to be strangled at the quarry. We had always been warned never to play at the quarry. I was a good enough girl who never went near the place, but I knew plenty of people who did. There was dark water in the bottom of the cutting.

The picture of Daphne comes up on my television when they decide to revisit some cold cases. A life chopped off at that moment when she stood by the curly iron gate. Her parents are dead now, but her brother, who was born soon after her death, appears on screen to appeal for information, memories, ideas – he reaches out of the screen and – how to explain it – he flicks a switch in my brain.

I have not been completely honest with you here. I have much to confess. I *can* explain what happens when Daphne's brother Gerald looks into my eyes and asks for help. I'm a clinical psychologist. I know what is going on.

Forgive me if I become a bit technical, but I want to be perfectly clear. Freud said that there was a force that stops people's memories of pathogenic experiences from becoming conscious, that compels the memories to remain unconscious. He called this repression. Repressed memories can sometimes be accessed. There are many triggers, often unexpected, and Gerald Harrower tripped my memory.

I am appalled at what I have remembered. How could I have forgotten? *How could I have forgotten?*

I am obliged to go to the police, for all the good it will do. It's nearly sixty years ago. Everybody's dead.

Well, not exactly everybody.

Here is the story I must tell to the police. I will tell them in the form of a report, a report in which I will be simply a reporter, and they will wonder, and they will ask me why I have never come forward before. Why didn't I report it at the time? They will just have to accept the fact that I had a pathogenic experience which forced the details to be buried in my unconscious.

But I need to tell you in the form of a story.

Miss Enid Pearl was my violin teacher. She lived in a pretty house at the end of the next street. It was like a house in a picture book, an ideal house with diamond leadlight windows and a heart shape cut into the front door. There was a brick path that led up to the door, winding between flower beds. A house for a fairy or a witch. Miss Pearl had a minute marmalade cat that sat on a Spanish shawl on the window-sill, and a canary in a cage. The canary was Robert, and the cat was Tatty. These details make her sound old and eccentric, but she was really quite young and pretty, and later on she married a clarinet player named George and they went to live in America.

Anyway, I had just perfected a simple piece, *Hirondelle*, and I was very pleased with myself. This was a year before the murder of Daphne Harrower, I would have been seven.

Picture this – I have severe plaits with navy blue ribbons on the ratty ends, and I'm wearing a panama hat and a navy blue school pinafore with a white blouse and a green and navy striped tie. My violin is in a wooden case like the coffin for a baby. My music books are in a leather case with my name stamped on it in gold. One case in each hand. I push open the low wooden gate with my knee, and walk carefully up the path, pausing now and then to consider the Fluffy-Ruffle petunias that line the path. They are striped rose, violet and white, and I stare down into their mysteriously veined throats. I am tempted to pick one. I can barely restrain myself. But I know this is forbidden. A violation of Miss Pearl's trust. I would like to kneel down and bury my nose in them. I know the perfume is subtle but delicious. We have Fluffy-Ruffles at home, but ours never seem to flourish and flounce in the way that Miss Pearl's always do. At the lesson I am praised for my work on *Hirondelle*, start on a new piece with the title *Alice, Where Art Thou?* When I have packed up, Miss Pearl walks with me down the brick path. We pause briefly to consider again the Fluffy-Ruffles, my lust for them barely contained, and then I am out the gate and we wave each other goodbye. See you next week.

Now I should explain that my love of flowers extended well past petunias, and I liked to take the long way home, wandering down past the big garden on the corner thick with rose bushes and pumpkin vines and fruit trees. This was a comfortable little part of the town, bright with flowers and story-books and sixpences in piggy-banks. I kept going. Along the gravel path, up the hill, around the next corner and the next. Until I came to a tall faded paling fence over which hung the burdened branches of the *Viburnum opulus Sterilis*. (I am trying to conceal from you, for purposes of suspense, the common name of this plant. It was, of course, the snowball bush.) Breathless pale green globes consisting of small florets, they seemed to hold bubbles of icy air within themselves.

I want to reach out and take one, cup it in my hands. Strange treasure. I put down the violin case, I put down the music case, I pinch my fingers around the base of the flower, but before I can tug or snip or tear, there is an animal roar of rage. The red face of an angry man, eyes popping, teeth bared, appears like a great fat wobbling scarecrow at the top of the fence.

'You touch that y'little bastard an' I'll git you an' I'll ram them bloody flowers down y' bloody throat!'

I grab the violin case and take to my heels, flying, leaving the music case behind.

I ran and ran until I reached our gate. I wept. I could never confess that I had gone off wandering, that I had tried to steal a flower, that I had heard the dreadful words the man said, that I had seen the man, that I had left my music case on the path. I was overwhelmed by my own guilt; I silenced myself; I repressed the details. Life went on.

'I lost my music case I don't know where I went for a walk I don't know I don't know.'

In due course the whole episode blew over. I got a new but inferior music case, and my mother always walked to Miss Pearl's with me. And back.

A few years later some boys found the music case in the shallow water at the bottom of the quarry. They brought it round to our house. It was rusted shut, and my father simply put it in the incinerator.

And now, thanks to cold case and television, I have the return of the repressed.

The red-faced man would be long dead.

But I am shaking with deep, deep shame. If I had confessed, had told my mother about the snowball bush and about the words the man shouted at me, would Daphne Harrower now be living happily somewhere in the world, famous for her botanical illustrations? Or perhaps she would be in a country town somewhere in Australia, with beds of petunias, pumpkin vines, and her very own *Viburnum opulus Sterilis* spilling its pale globes over the fence and into the blue-green air.

Cactus

Massage and Mystical Vibrations Has/Have Closed. Wanda and Craig. They argued about the verb. Should it be singular or plural. Hard to say really. Neither of them could decide. Then they tried *Massage and Mystical Vibrations. Closed.* That seemed OK. So he printed it out in some weird font or other, huge, purple, and stuck it inside the glass on the front door with a picture of a sort of sexy angel. It was the end of dreams, end of what could be called an era. Close of business. Where to from here, though. Let's think. The Victorian town was rural, tiny, very tiny. Once, well this was long ago, back in what century – the nineteenth – there had been fifteen pubs. That's how they tell it, how they judge the size of the town back when there was gold – was there gold – all over the place. The Fox and Hounds, the Queen's Head, the Pig and Whistle – that sort of thing.

There's still two left – the Travellers Rest, no apostrophe, the Mermaid Tavern. Not that there are many travellers these days, and there's never been a mermaid. Ever. It was nostalgia then, and now it's nostalgia for nostalgia. Four handsome brick churches of four different kinds, now sold off to folks from elsewhere seeking rural charm and something different with cathedral ceilings and maybe a ghost in the crypt. Stained glass windows glowing with pictures of St Agnes plus lamb, St Catherine plus wheel, Mary and Jesus on a donkey, sacred to the memory of Julius Dent, Wilhelmina Robinson and other prominent members of the old community. And anyhow, Craig and Wanda opened Massage and Mystical Vibrations in joyful expectation that seekers after truth would come wending their way to the tiny little old town where the creek once ran, if you believe the stories, with flecks of golden gold. Well it must have, mustn't it, because of all those pubs and those four lovely churches, red brick pointed in sandstone, warm and golden and ghostly. These days the banks of the creek are a sea of some sort of huge and threatening cactus, and there's a woman in a small blue caravan under the willow tree. Yellow cactus flowers joyous in the summer. Rivers of a kind of pale gold. Talk about spines! The woman in the caravan is Xenia, and she takes all kinds of clients from far and wide across the region and beyond, several discreet gentlemen coming, from time to time, from the city. She's a legend. Well, the hope was that people would also keep coming for Craig's Miraculous Massage, for Wanda's Violet Vibrations – which involved crystals and incense and the quiet mysterious music of whales and wind. Her brother Ryan used to come in on Fridays to do the tattoos. But that finished up when he was put away for dealing. You two are so naïve, people said, of course he was doing drugs, he was using you, what do you think he was up to in the back room on the phone day and night. From time to time, strange men with rings and sunglasses drifted silently by at four o'clock in the afternoon, driving silver cars and muttering. Talk about clichés! Those men would cruise around the town, peering casually at the solid grandeur of the three old banks, the lyrical splendour of the churches, in particular the Presbyterian, and would settle in the corner of the Mermaid for a quiet vodka and orange before slithering out onto the road again, and back to the city. Brazen they were, in their way. One of them occasionally paid Xenia a visit. But they never showed up again, after Ryan was busted. Ryan could ink a fabulous angel on your forearm, or a devil on your backside. He went away at about the time the seekers after truth started to stop coming. It was just coincidence. Same time Wanda had baby Tatiana, and just after the flood which was described in the city papers as being positively Biblical. Like the fires ten years before. Now the waters lapped at the foundations of Massage and Mystical, but in the end all was safe and sound and high and dry. High and dry with the business failing and nobody seeking truth through massage and vibration any more. So Wanda and Craig came to a kind of decision and they printed out the notice in the purple font with the angel and stuck it on the door and then they sat down on the floor and stared at each other while the CD of the whales played softly in the Vibration Room, and the aromatic candles burned in a kind of holy way on a low glass table. Baby Tatiana was asleep in her cot which was made, as it happened, from something resembling bullrushes. In fact

Craig and Wanda owned the premises outright, that's a surprise. How come? Oh, it had been in the family since way back, way back when Craig's great great grandfather William set up shop as a blacksmith, back when the pubs were pubs and the churches were churches and there was gold in the creek and no cactus. Although there had always been, since time immemorial, a woman in a caravan down by the creek.

Do you think we should sell up and move?

Where would we go?

Queensland. Or California. Let's go to California.

What would we do in California?

Go swimming. Open up again, in one of those old mission places.

Don't you have to get a Green Card?

Ryan knows a place where you can get a Green Card.

Ryan's not much use right now.

That's where you're wrong, see. He's got more contacts now he's on the inside.

In fact Ryan did have the contacts, and so Wanda and Craig got their Green Cards, and they sold the premises for a dazzling sum to the Maxwells, a retired couple in their sixties who had fallen in love with the town, and who planned to renovate and extend and breed Staffies. They brought their amazing antique furniture with them, Louis XVl and so forth, chandeliers, paintings, bedheads, and Wanda and Craig and baby Tatiana set sail – well took off – for California where, in the old mission towns, people continue to seek after truth, and sometimes there are fires, and sometimes there are floods, and there is always a woman in a caravan. And cactus too, yes, cactus with all kinds of flowers shooting out between the spines, yellow, red and purple, all triumphant in the legendary sunlight of the Californian coast.

The Matter of the Mosque

Week One: Hairspray or Mousse

Carly and Tara and Kelly are sitting on the floor. Each has a brush in her hand, and they are all brushing their little daughters' hair. The children sit with heads bowed, very still, legs crossed, hands gripping their feet. The feet are in pale pink ballet slippers. Legs covered with the powdery cloth of ballet tights. Silky black leotards, skimpy skirts, crossover tops with long sleeves concealing skinny little arms.

'Sometimes, I can't decide which is better, hairspray or mousse,' Carly says. Her daughter Peyton shifts a fraction sideways on the carpet.

'I know. Sometimes I reckon it's the spray,' says Tara as she slowly draws the brush from Nevaeh's forehead towards the centre of her skull.

'I love spray,' says Kelly, holding the brush in the air above Cadence's head.

Sunlight entering in strips through the half-closed slat blind, falls on the hands and the hairbrushes, and on the smooth round surfaces of the children's heads. All heads glint dark gold. There could be a halo around one of the heads.

More small girls flutter in with their mothers. One father. He's a paramedic. The air in the room wriggles and shifts while he unzips his daughter's jacket, and positions the child on the floor where she waits quietly for the door to the studio to open. He leaves, a handsome shape in navy blue with badges.

Week Two: The Blazer and the Common Cold

'So is Cadence going to Vincent Street next year?'

'Yes, we enrolled. They're restoring the old assembly hall.'

'So they'll all be at school together then.'

'Did you get the uniform list?'

'I did. Now I need to get the name tags done. How many prep classes are there?'

'Two I think.'

'I like the summer dress, don't you?'

'It's OK I suppose. How about the blazer though? Why do they have to have that great big blazer?'

'Yes it's so expensive.'

'And thick and heavy.'

'Good in the winter.'

'Not as good as a fleece. In my opinion.'

'It's traditional. They've always had it. I went to Vincent Street. We had the blazer.'

'Same thing?'

'Exactly the same thing. I hated it.'

'Has Peyton got a cold then?'

'They all have. Mum had it and they all got it.'

'Nevaeh's had one all the winter.'

'Cadence seems to have a permanent sniffle. I don't know.'

The other mothers and children are wafting in. Snot running out of noses. The paramedic comes, ruffles the edges of the air, leaves his daughter, and goes.

'Is your mum making the cake for Cadence's party?'

'She's already done it. It's Elsa. She had to cut the legs off the doll.'

'Well she would I suppose.'

'She left them on the table at my place and the cat decided to play with them.'

'You ought to throw them out.'

'Oh I will. But everything's pretty hectic. My sister just had twins. Boy and girl.'

'God! But she already had twins.'

'I know. Crazy isn't it?'

'What'd she call them this time?'

'She's into magic and goddesses and stuff.'

'So what'd she call them?

'Jataya and Isis. One's an Indian eagle man and the other one's Egyptian. I think. A goddess.'

'Really pretty. Where's the party?'

'Its going to be at Scallywags. Peyton'll get an invitation. And Cadence. We're actually sending them in the mail. Old style.'

'Nice.'

Other mothers, children, paramedic, coming and going.

Week Four: Costumes and The Matter of the Mosque

'So did you get the costumes for the concert?'

'Yes, Peyton's is a bit big.'

'Same here.'

'I got mum to take it in a bit.'

'I thought I'd do that too.'

'Cadence is always looking in the mirror at home, doing the doll dance.'

'Yes, they love the doll dance.'

'You live round the corner, don't you, from the – ah – mosque.'

'We'll have to move of course. They park all over the nature strip. Blocking the drive. And those prayer calls all the time. Waking up the children, setting off the dogs.'

'And the way they treat women.'

'AK-47s.'

'Well, yes. You only have to watch the news to see what they're like.'

'No way they're getting their hands on *our* girls.'

Raping, murdering, hacking off heads, guns, those sword things, bombing, looting, executing innocent children. Ours was a peaceful neighbour-hood until they got their fucking bloody hands on everything in sight. Terrorists. We have to move. God knows where we'll go. Moving's so expensive too. Torture. Raping and murdering and hacking to death. Hacking, raping, torturing, raping children. Women. Hacking off heads.

Mothers, children, paramedic.

Week Five: Nothing Works for Nits

'I need to warn you, Cadence's got nits. Everyone at her kinda's got them. I've tried everything.'

'Only thing that works is using the comb and squashing them with your fingers. I've spent hours.'

'Me too. Hours.'

'Of course we can't cut their hair because of ballet, can we.'

'Right.'

'There's nothing you can do.

'Nothing.'

'I thought maybe hairspray would help.'

'Not really.'

'No, nothing helps.'

Carly and Tara and Kelly are sitting on the floor. They are brushing the children's hair until it is smooth and can be twisted into a tight, tight bun. Then they wind a filmy net around the bun and jab in several golden pins. Other children drift in. Other mothers. A handsome paramedic and his daughter. Sunlight slants through the slats of the blind, falls on the heads of the children. Glints. Halo. Like a blessing.

Surrogate

Once upon a time – well no – it was in Hobart in the early fifties, if you can imagine that at all. It might as well be once upon a time. This began before television. Not that that matters really, but I suppose it means that for one thing the people in the story spent no time at all lying on the sofa eating ice cream, drinking beer. Naturally they did eat ice cream and drink beer – they weren't completely uncivilized. They were quite respectable and presentable. The leader of their state was, as it happened, a left-wing fellow, whereas the whole country was led by a tall silver-haired right-wing man who had been leader for as long as anyone could remember. What I am trying to say is that things were generally pleasant and stable. And Silver Hair described such people as those in the story as *the backbone of post-war Australia.*

And they were. Respectable, presentable back-bones of post-war Australia.

There were the Spines and the Backbones, and they lived next door to each other. This is a story about neighbours. Such stories can have happy endings, but not necessarily. Ron and Angela Spine and their teenage children Neal and Prudence in the one house, and Hans and Matty Backbone, who had no family, in the next. By their first names you can possibly tell that Hans and Matty had come from the Netherlands on what was known as the *second wave* of immigration. Hans had been a boat-builder and Matty had been a midwife. But this was a new life, here in Hobart. Everything was different. Hans had a job in a small grocery store. Nostalgic for home, Hans and Matty began to call Prudence, who was as pretty as a flower, Tulip. And it stuck. Everybody started calling her Tulip. Pretty she might have been, and charming, but she was also empty-headed. Neal was brighter, and got a job in an office. His father worked in an office. His mother was a housewife who worked day and night in the home, which was as neat as a new pin. You should have seen the sparkle on her window panes, for one thing.

She was a genius knitter, and not only knitted the sample garments – complicated sweaters and cardigans for all ages – for the woollen mills, but she modelled them as well. Angela Spine was a familiar face in pattern books and magazine advertisements, showing off the fruits of her labours, and the labours of hundreds of other women with knitting needles. She had always been pretty, with a good figure. Smiling with respectable teeth into the respectable camera. Clothed in soft wool that had been worked into patterns of such intricacy it is a marvel the human brain could even devise them, let alone transfer them by needle and finger and yarn into objects more marvelous than the web of a spider.

It was only natural that from babyhood Tulip would follow Angela into the pattern books. Not that Tulip was a knitter – remember her empty head. She didn't have the brains for it. But she was the perfect face and form from the beginning, right from babyhood. And don't forget that Tasmania was famous for wool, and that Australia generally was riding high on the sheep's back. It was possibly Silver Hair who thought up that particular image.

So there they were, the Spines, smooth and happy in their new pin house with vegetable garden and chickens and dog and small car and wool and needles everywhere. That sounds untidy. No, the wool and so forth was all neatly filed in two large chests of drawers in a tiny room called the sewing room where there was a treadle sewing machine and an ironing board that came miraculously out of the wall when it was needed. Angela was also a seamstress and an embroiderer. And of course she was a good plain cook. You can see she was something of a treasure. The whole family riding, as it were, on the sheep's back.

And then came the Backbones, speaking surprisingly good English, to live in the little old cottage next door, to transform the large block of land with rows of cherry trees and beds of tulips, to fill the air with the perfume of speculoos – call them windmill cookies – and generally with the warm aromas of cinnamon and chocolate and vanilla. In the front garden of the Backbones' cottage was an ancient mulberry tree so that the little house with its red window-sills and tiny green door nestled away beneath and behind deep green shade. In the back garden was an aviary where Hans kept finches – zebras, crimsons, diamond firetails – all kinds of seed-eating songbirds. Tall blonde Hans was gentle and loving, a sight to behold among the birds in his aviary. Matty was a busy little fat woman – young but plump – in a large apron. She worked two nights a week in a bakery, introducing, as time went on, lovely Dutch things to the shelves, to the delight and amazement of the local people.

Now I said Tulip was empty-headed, but what I really meant was that she was what was known as *mildly retarded*, and although she was very attractive to boys, she was in fact afraid of them. This fear had been instilled by Angela who harboured a wish that her daughter might magically marry a kind and nurturing man of modest wealth and general respectability. Tulip had to be kept close. Posing in lacey cardigans, smiling on demand. Adorable. Blonde curls, blue eyes. Shirley Temple adorable.

In due course, after spending days in Matty's kitchen inhaling the aroma of the speculoos, out in the garden feeding the finches, even weeding the flowerbeds and picking the cherries, Tulip became almost like one of the Backbone family, who had come sailing in on the second wave.

Now you will remember that Matty and Hans had no children. They began to explore the possibility of adopting a baby, but they were a long long way down the list. In the meantime Tulip was almost like the daughter they did not have. Matty loved to brush her hair and tie it up in strangely Dutch pigtails.

In reality, it was all considerably deeper and darker than that, there beneath and behind the shade of mulberry tree. You knew it would be. Matty and Hans believed – with good reason as it happened – that whereas Matty was infertile, Hans was not. Matty, as they say, was the problem. And so between them they devised a curious plan. Perhaps Tulip could have a baby for them!! If Tulip would go to bed with Hans, she could have a baby and they, the Backbones, could pretend it was theirs. You can see that they were carried away by the idea, and were not quite thinking it through. Although they weren't quite as silly as they sound. And in their wisdom and industry they had begun to amass a little fortune, had begun their own ride on the back of the sheep. They would offer to make Tulip their heir – after the baby of course. He – it would be a boy – would be the greater beneficiary. Tulip the heiress would be the lesser. There are many flaws in this plan, as you can see, not the least of which being the possibility of a girl baby. As I say, they were not really thinking, so carried away were they with the whole idea.

I have to say that Hans was particularly keen on the notion of going to bed with Tulip. But that might be another matter. Or might it?

Trust. What they had developed in good faith with the Spines was a trusting neighbourly relationship – long words like that may well set off the alarm bells for you. Yes, a trusting neighbourly relationship had developed.

As can often happen in a story, Angela, Tulip's mother, fell ill and died. The good mother, gone. The pretty daughter, unprotected. You might ask what her brother and father were doing about all this, but they, I am sorry to tell you, lived in another world – yes – a world of the office and the car and the cricket and the vegetable garden and a beer on special occasions. Neal was going to marry a girl from the office, whatsmore, so he was fully occupied and blind. Also television had at last come, so any blank moments which Neal might have given to intelligent thought, were nicely filled. He took up the beer and ice cream thing, I have to say.

Tulip is lost without Angela. Tulip is out on a limb. Or in limbo. Vulnerable and ripe.

How terrible that the benign cookie-cooking cherry-picking finch-feeding Backbones have turned out to be the villains of the piece. It happens.

And so it was that one day, one fine day in Hobart when the sun was shining on the water, and television had come to the land, Matty prepared the bedroom with sweet scented pillows. She put a vase of white daisies on the dressing table. It wasn't exactly a chamber fit for a princess, but neither was it a bordello. All was crisp and soft and white and special.

Hans and Tulip feed the birds and come into the kitchen for coffee and cookies. Tulip chattering like a crimson finch. As usual. But Matty is not there at the stove. She has gone off on her bicycle to fetch some flour, says Hans. And little by little he shifts Tulip from the kitchen to the bedroom where, as it turns out, she is only too willing to do his bidding. She forgets all about Matty. So, as it happens, does Hans. No surprise there.

That was the first time. That was the beginning. The whole thing quickly developed into a love affair. Oh no – not a love affair! This was meant to be business of a kind. Well, it was business of a kind.

It wasn't quite what Matty had expected. Life can be so complicated, can't it. Knitting patterns are one thing; life is altogether another. But Matty still wants the child – time enough to work out what to do about Tulip after the boy is born. Yes, time enough.

Ron can't see what is going on under his nose. Neal isn't really present. Tulip is on her own.

When she was three months pregnant, Matty the midwife took over the management of things. She explained to Tulip that the baby would belong to Matty and Hans, and that because they were grateful to her, they would leave her a lot of money when they died. Hans took on the incredibly difficult job of explaining the matter to Ron.

Ron, as it happened, was having a perfectly delicious courtship of another neighbour called Ruth.

Who would have picked him for a romantic? So, what with his usual state of mind, and the added magic of love, he was in no fit condition to deal rationally with what Hans was telling him. There are fairy stories, aren't there, where there are characters called Clever Hans. I think perhaps Hans Backbone was one of those. He sold the idea to Ron. Tulip would be taken care of for life.

Tulip ate sensible food; Matty knitted baby clothes. She was possibly more gifted with her knitting than even Angela. Around the hem of the matinee jacket, and around the face of the tiny bonnet, she knitted a joyful flight of bluebirds. Tulip was sent away to stay with some Dutch people in the north of the island, far enough from the other neighbours in that respectable street in Hobart. Matty travelled north for the last month of the pregnancy, leaving Hans at home with the flowers and the finches and so forth. He felt a strange kind of relief. Peace and quiet. He loved the garden. The cherries were ripening and he had to construct wire cages for them, to keep out the blackbirds. He also made a beautiful cradle from golden wood. Matty was kind and loving to Tulip, and everyone was happy in expectation of the great event.

And in the fullness of time Tulip gave birth to a baby girl. What did I say – yes – a baby girl. Matty experienced some disappointment at the sight, but was in fact filled with joy at the very manifestation of a living child. Hans, somewhat downcast, feeling no joy at all, registered the birth, claiming Bellina as the child of Matty and Hans Backbone. Done!

Matty came back home with her baby daughter. Tulip came home to Neal and Ruth – the whole thing almost ruined the romance between those two. For one thing Ruth found the whole business shocking and repellant, and for another she didn't want Tulip around anyway. So there's Tulip out on that limb. Again. Although Hans wouldn't have minded if she lived with the Backbones, Matty was definitely against it. Things drifted on for a while there, until it began to dawn on Hans and Matty that baby Bellina was strange. The truth of the matter is that Bellina suffered from – I'll give you the scientific name here – achondroplasia. This means that she was a dwarf.

Matty wished to keep her – she was her only chance at the motherhood she so longed for. But Hans was beside himself with horror. Not just a girl, but a dwarf girl. He turned on Tulip in rage, a rage such as she had never imagined possible in any human being. You must have been able to hear him shouting in Dutch for miles around. He threatened to kill her and to kill Bellina with her. Yes, beside himself with rage.

The story – I think I suggested earlier that it wasn't going to be happy – ends with what is called a *murder-suicide*. For in the dead of night Tulip bundled up Bellina in a shawl as fine as spider web, a shawl that Angela had once knitted for Tulip herself, and ran and ran into the darkness, stumbling past houses glowing with television, pausing for breath at the crossroads. Running, running. What else could she do? But where to go?

The two of them were found the next day floating in the river, not so very far from home.

My tale is done, there runs a mouse; whosoever catches it, may make from it a big fur cap.

Letter to Lola

Melância Creek, Bahia, Brazil

Christmas Eve 2000

Lola, My Lovely,

Forgive me for writing this letter on the reverse of a fragment of the Basurto dinner party invitation. Alas, this is all I have to hand. I know you will understand, my darling. Here in the backlands of the disappearing green fringes of the caraiba forests, paper is scarce. I write with bright pink juice from the cadaver of a goat, knowing the colour will please you. My instrument is a spine from a fat old cactus. Today, in memory of you, I have feasted well on the seeds and juices of your favourite faveleira. My thoughts have been filled, as they forever are, with pictures and sounds of you, my dearest Lola, my childhood sweetheart, my own.

My rational mind tells me that you have gone, have gone; yet in my heart of heart I hold you still, beloved, and I know that you will hear my lovesong as I write to you, you in your resting place in the great beyond.

I recall the joyful days when, together as one, we steered our course, our long blue tails flexed against the air, through the tip tops of the caraiba. I recall how we would come to rest, almost floating into the ancient family home. There in the nest chamber you tended our three rare and precious unhatched chicklings. Deep inside the hollow of our tree.

Then there flashes upon me the memory of the dark edge of doom. In the eerie light before the dawn, the drone of the vehicle. The trappers. We huddle together. The trappers whisper as they scratch and scrape at the walls of our house. The gloved hand – then the arm enters, feeling for you, for me, for the eggs. Like fine thin glass the pure white shells are shattered. The yolks, blood-streaked, flow and drip into the bottom of the nest. You clamber up, heading for the exit, the circle of faint light as the radiance of the pre-dawn leads you on toward freedom. I follow. You spread your darling wings. You enter the net that awaits you.

In the horror of panic, with my heart pounding, there was nought for me to do but struggle past. Forgive me, forgive me, my own, for I could not save you, although I saved myself. I flew in blind desperation into the trees, away.

All this happened exactly thirteen years ago, on Christmas Eve, 1987, my blue bird of eternal happiness and sorrow. I write this letter to tell you of my love for you, and also to set down the sad and complicated story of our lives. As daylight came and you lay in your dreadful cage in terror, a cheerful and curious stranger approached the trappers on foot. They showed him their prize, my lovely, my Lola, and with his Polaroid camera he took a picture. There it was, gradually forming on the paper, an image – pale grey head, great black beak, sharp yellow eyes, brilliant turquoise dress feathers, and your long, long blue tail – it was you. The last wild girl ever, captured and sold into the slavery of the zoos. It was three years before the scientists, seeking our kind in the wild, saw this picture and realized they were looking at you, the last, my last, wild girl. They played their tape recordings of our call, played our music to your Polariod, my love.

I was alone in the forest. I searched for you, I flew on and on and I sought you, I sought you down the nights and down the days, down the years and years in baking sunshine and when rain fell upon the earth. I could never have imagined such loneliness, such sorrow, such despair. You were the last wild girl, I the last wild boy.

Those scientists who came to the caraiba forest in 1990, they sighted me, the lone bird, in the early daylight, and they gazed at me through their binoculars, and they filmed me with their video cameras. I called for you, and they recorded my sad call. *Kraa, kraa, kraa.* Should they capture me, they wondered? Should they? It took them two more years to decide that they would leave me in the wild. But they had interesting plans. A miracle was about to occur.

After my seven sorrowful years of solitude, of being apart from you, my rarest, my most beautiful, my most coveted Lola, in 1995, suddenly, among the dappled light and shade of the waxy caraiba leaves, *you were there*. Not the dancing hallucination of my dreams, but the long lost shimmering, gleaming turquoise princess of my days. They had released you, given you back to me.

Unable to believe what had occurred, we flew in an ecstatic and bewildered trance, feasting not only on the faveleira trees, but also on delicious pinhão and juicy joazeiro. The short three months we were together remain the strangest, the brightest, and ultimately the saddest months of my life. This time you were not stolen, my lovely Lola. You flew, my dearest, by accident into the invisible new electric power lines, and were killed. I can scarcely believe the bitter cruelty of fate. I mourn for you for all eternity.

I must confess to you, my own, that my lasting faithfulness to you has, over the years, been spoiled yet not dimmed. For in my loneliness I have sometimes had the companionship of our cousin, Linda, the little green maracana. I knew her slightly during my seven years of isolation, and yes she sometimes joined us on our journeys in 1995. Forgive me. Perhaps you do not wish to know the rest of the story. We flew together,

Linda and I, in the daylight, and usually I took her back to her own family at night. I slept alone on the top of a prickly cactus. And I defended our old home from the many others who wished to colonise it. In 1996, the year after I saw you, my lovely, for the last time, Linda and I moved in, and there were three eggs, but even they were stolen. In 1999 the scientists brought for us some eggs from my cousins in a zoo. With great joy we hatched them, and they flew with us. I do not know where those children are now. Naturally, I fear for them, knowing what I know. Linda and I have now parted company.

It is thirteen years, or five thousand days and nights since first you were stolen away from me, only to return for those three brief months of joyful life. On this Christmas Eve, the first of the new century, I am secretly at large, undetected by the scientists and the trappers. I fly on in lonely longing, writing this letter to you on the sad anniversary of the time when first I lost you.

I shall but love thee better after death,
Your ever devoted
Spix.

Reference: Spix's Macaw – The Race to Save the World's Rarest Bird by Tony Juniper, Fourth Estate 2003

The Tale of the Last Unicorn

Believe me, Best Beloved, I am the last of my kind. I am not sure whether to say the last of my family, tribe or species. It is really species, I believe. In any case, I have retired. Here in the far south-west forest of unimaginable beauty and secret depth – I refer to the impenetrable virgin woods of Van Diemen's Land – I plan to spend eternity. Now there is a somewhat marvellous concept, eternity. I understand it but I am unable to explain it. I think about it – being the last unicorn, I think about it a lot. In my thoughts and dreams I go drifting back to the beginning, but then the concept of the beginning is also no simple thing to explain, however I may be able to describe it. Bear in mind the fact that I am probably seven hundred years old. At least.

Once upon a time, the universe, if there was a universe, lay deep in slumber, dreaming of the beginning and the end, outside time, beyond space, just dreaming. There was no time, there was no space; there was dreaming, dreaming and sleeping, and no sound. Nothing was happening. But somehow, in this sleeping, dreaming, sound-less stillness, something stirred. Or so I have been told. As I have indicated, my understanding is primitive, but I believe that by accident or by design, there came into being particles of light. And these particles of light dreamt their way together, and they must have collided, shat-tered, must have split into a million million tiny shards, shards of what can only be described these days as colours. Now if you can imagine a rope, twisted twine, plaited from all the colours in all their permutations and perambulations, you can begin to visualize the embodiment of the vast all-coloured female – for females as you know are very keen on colours. Yes, it was a female serpent. The first of her kind, well, to tell you the truth, she was the only one of her kind. Unique. Like me. I am the last and she was the first, and here we are now, in the woods of Van Diemen's Land. You thought I was alone; I did not mean to mislead you – I have the company of the Serpent, and we are known among ourselves – and we have only ourselves – as Unie and Serpie, or US.

Serpie has done incredible work in her time – and I do not mean to imply that her time is up – for US, time, you see, does not exist. Things are more or less as they were before the dreaming. There is no time as such, although throughout the earth all the creatures of sea and land and air, and also all the plants, all the seasons, are still moving and shining and kind of billowing as they perform the dreaming which goes on for eternity. There I go again, eternity. But I am attempting to describe the beginning, am I not.

Others have given me their accounts of the beginning, but the one I trust is Serpie who has the beguiling voice of a mother telling fairy tales at bedtime. She says that she herself was the beginning, the mother of every living thing, emerging from the virtual nothingness in all her dazzling hues, and winding her way all over – all over! – the earth leaving sweet indentations and hollows until she finally returned to the first fissure, or place of her birth, and she suddenly found the ability to speak, to call, to conjure up another living creature. She called, and from the fissure, which had grown wide and weird in the time she had been away, leapt a whole family of bright green frogs! And she tickled them and soon they were laughing and leaping and gurgling and carrying on. And off they went all over the earth where lakes and waterways and seas appeared, and so came plants. Then out from the fissure which was now enormous flocked all sorts and kinds of animals – even birds and fish and so forth. Butterflies and bees. Imagine. And unicorns, naturally. And when it was ticking along nicely, Serpie sorted it all out with her rules and regulations, and any creature that disobeyed her was – wait for it – turned to stone. This was good because it gave rise to mountains and valleys, and they are very useful in their way. I've been up to the top of some very high mountains, and I can tell you that the sight of the earth from up there truly is an inspiration!

It all sounds quite good, doesn't it, Beloved. But you must have begun to wonder, then, why Serpie and I have retired to the deep dark forest here at the End of the Earth.

All is not well in the world, and as I said, I am the last of my tribe. Serpie has got eternity in hand for herself, and she assures me she will extend it to me as well. Such power and generosity! She needs the company she says; it is extremely lonely here. And dark. Oh yes, it is very very dark. It so happens that the usual systems of the earth are shutting down one by one. Plague, droughts, floods, fires, famines. And the earth appears to have lost the will to regenerate. The lights are going out, I have heard, all over Europe. Oh, I remember Europe with such great affection. There was a time when I got to know the prettiest girls in France, Italy, Spain – those joyful bounteous countries lapped by the waters of the blue blue Mediterranean. Men on horseback with dogs and trumpets would spend their afternoons hunting for me in the forest. They would sit a pale and beautiful and spotless lady, young and tender, on a little silken seat in a glade where flowers dotted the grasses like red and orange stars. And they would imagine I would lie in the lap of the lady, overcome with enchantment. Then, they thought, they could shoot me with their arrows, and catch me in their nets, and – well I never really knew the end of the story – I think they planned to kill me and eat me. Eat me? Was that it? At a banquet in the vast hall of the nearby castle under the indigo sky?

I have heard tell that this is how many of my brothers met their fate, but I never knew what really happened when the men took the bodies back to the castle. I believe they used to keep the horn.

However in my own case, it was thus:

I lived in the deepest part of the Forest of Paimpont where lie the Tomb of Merlin, the Fountain of Youth, and the castle of the Lady of the Lake. One day when I was very young, white as milk and soft as a baby swan, I was strolling carelessly through the dappled light beneath the great oaks and beeches, when I saw, sitting very still in a pool of sunlight, a girl in a bright yellow – you might say golden – cloak. There were jewels in her hair. Her sweet head was tilted up to the sun, and I saw that she was blind. And she was weeping. Slowly, very slowly, I tiptoed up to her, and from behind the trunk of a vast and noble oak tree I whispered: 'Why do you weep, fair lady, why do you weep?' She drew in her breath and lowered her sightless gaze, moving her shoulders in a little shuddering gesture. I spoke again: 'Why do you weep?'

'My brothers have placed me here to die,' she said, in the voice of resignation and regret.

'I must die because of my blindness. No man will marry me, and I must die. Wolves will come and eat me. And so I weep.'

'If you will sit upon my back,' I said, 'I will lead you far away to a place of safety where your brothers will never ever find you. Will you come with me?'

'But who are you?'

I told her I was the youngest local unicorn, and she started up in alarm.

'But you must flee!' she said. 'Fly from this place because my brothers are out hunting, and they will kill you also.'

'Then,' I said, 'we must flee together.'

And we did, Best Beloved, we did. We journeyed for three nights and three days through rain and shine until we came to the lodging of an honest carpenter who offered us water and food and shelter. His wife gave the lady some sandals and a plain brown garment, for the lady had lost her slippers and her yellow cloak, and her green and violet silken dress was now in tatters. And do you know, we lived there in safety and happiness, meeting, from time to time, other pale and noble ladies from castles far away, ladies who were escaping from their brothers, husbands, convents. Until a great sickness swept over the land, and on one terrible, bleak afternoon the carpenter, the wife, their five little children and the lady all took the fever, and all died.

It was then that I began my lifelong dangerous journey across the dear planet on strange and untrustworthy vessels, over centuries, over seas, until I came at last, in recent times, to this haven at the End of the Earth where I met for the first time my dear and colourful companion Serpie who will take me with her into the great unknown forests of eternity.

That is the end of my telling of the tale, but the tale will go on and on until what is sometimes called *forever and a day*. Here we dwell in forest darkness, just US, at the End of the Earth, Forever and a Day.

Acknowledgments

The following stories have been previously published:

'The Dead Aviatrix', 'Surrogate' (*Southerly*);

'Cactus', 'Cold Case' (*Review of Australian Fiction*);

'The Matter of the Mosque' (*Antipodes*);

'The Tale of the Last Unicorn' (*Island Magazine*);

'Dear Lola' (*Australian Short Stories*).

Biography

CARMEL BIRD is the 2016 winner of the Patrick White Literary Award. Carmel's work spans forty years, and she has published thirty-eight books. Her most recent collection, published in 2015, is *My Hearts Are Your Hearts,* and the most recent of her eleven novels is *Field of Poppies,* published in 2019.

Carmel's key work on memoir is *Writing the Story of Your Life* and her classic book on writing short fiction has been recently updated as *Dear Writer Revisited.* Two of her anthologies, *The Penguin Century of Australian Stories* and *The Stolen Children – Their Stories* mark significant milestones in Australian literary history.

Carmel's work is known for its lightness of touch, coupled with a seriousness of purpose, some of her concerns being the history of Australia's First Peoples, reproductive technology, loss of species, lost children. Language, the construction of fiction, and book design are some of her key preoccupations.

Find more of her writing at www.carmelbird.com

Praise for Carmel Bird

'Carmel Bird's short stories are ingenious, each a delicious fictional Venus fly trap that encloses you in its wonder or horror, or both. There is little terrain of the human condition that her stories don't touch – a child's cold case murder and a triggered memory that may have solved it, the sinister banality of suburban life and all its hidden vestibules, beauty and ugliness, creation and the future of the world, small towns and their dark undercurrents, and of course love. Bird's stories fizz and tingle with originality and freshness, and carry an alluring humour that can turn malevolent and deadly in the blink of an eye. Hands down, Carmel Bird is to my mind the best living short story writer in the country.'

– Matthew Condon

'Bird's imagination is extraordinarily wide-ranging and her fiction consequently creates a world that criss-crosses textual, intellectual and geographical boundaries. Her philosophical enquiry gives us stories that blend genres and also question faith and spirituality as well as personal, family and local history. Using elements of the Gothic, fantasy and fairy tale as easily as realism, Bird can be surreal, quirky and macabre, but also humorous, humane and warm. Critics have noted these qualities shared with other celebrated writers such as Angela Carter and Thea Astley, and at least one has identified a 'rogue quality' in her work reminiscent of Kurt Vonnegut and Gabriel Garcia Marquez. But Bird's voice is truly original: witty, stylish and allusive, it invests trust in the reader to appreciate her literary and cultural references.'

    – From Judges' Report; The 2016 Patrick White Award

'Carmel Bird's stories are dark, intriguing and yet always delightful.'
      – Andy Griffiths

'As you'd expect, Bird's beautiful stories soar, though never into a realm you could anticipate.'
      – Debra Adelaide

About This Collection

The Dead Aviatrix: Eight Short Stories by Carmel Bird was first published in the Spineless Wonders Capsule Collection Series. This series was a platform for digital-first collections of short stories, as well as for verse novels and novellas.

The collection is now part of the Spineless Wonders Smalls series of small format paperbacks published to celebrate our tenth year in publishing.

To find out about other books published in this series, go to www.shortaustralianstories.com.au

About This Series

The Dead Aviatrix by Carmel Bird is published as part of the Spineless Wonders Smalls series of small format paperbacks released to celebrate our tenth year in publishing.

To find out about other books published in this series, go to www.shortaustralianstories.com.au